READING CHAMPION

The Sleepover

by Jenny Jinks and Louise Forshaw

W
FRANKLIN WATTS
LONDON • SYDNEY

Grace had been waiting for this day
to come for weeks. She was going to
her friend Maya's house for a sleepover.
It was her first sleepover, and she was
very excited.

"Is it time to go yet?" she asked.

"No, not yet," laughed Mum.

"Finish your breakfast first.

Then we'll go and pack your things."

After breakfast, Grace rushed up to
her room and looked in the drawer.
What should she take? She didn't want to
forget anything. She started to put
things into a bag.

Mum laughed when she saw the bag.

"You can't take all of that!" she said.

"But I need it all," said Grace.

"I need my pyjamas and my toothbrush.

I need a torch for when it's dark and ..."

Grace stopped and looked at Mum.

"What's the matter?" said Mum.

"What if I don't like it at Maya's house?" said Grace. "I like playing superheroes, but Maya likes riding her bike."

"Maybe you can take turns to choose what to play," said Mum.

That made Grace feel a bit happier.

At lunchtime, Grace looked worried again.

"What if there's spaghetti for dinner?"

she said. "I hate spaghetti."

Mum smiled. "Don't worry," she said.

"Maya's mum knows you hate spaghetti.

She told me you're going to have pizza."

"I like pizza," said Grace, and she smiled.

After lunch, Grace asked, "What else

will we play at Maya's house?"

"You like playing football," said Mum.

"Perhaps you can play football together."

"I love football!" said Grace. "But Maya

likes doing handstands."

"Then she can teach you to do handstands.

And you can teach her some football tricks,"

said Mum.

When it was time to go, Grace and Mum

went upstairs to get the bag.

"You can take turns playing games,

and you like pizza for dinner," said Mum.

"You'll have lots of fun."

"Maybe," said Grace. But then she frowned.

"What about bedtime? I can't go to sleep

without Flop. Who will hug me goodnight?"

"Flop can come with you," said Mum.

"And I will fill him up with goodnight hugs

before I put him in the bag."

Grace felt much better.

Mum and Grace went to Maya's house.

Maya ran out to meet them.

"We're going to have fun!" Maya said.

"We're going to dress up, go on the bikes,

do handstands and play football.

And Mum says we can have a midnight feast!"

"I can't wait!" said Grace.

Grace had fun playing with Maya.

They dressed up and went on the bikes.

They did handstands and played football.

They had pizza for dinner and

Grace felt happy.

But at bedtime, Grace started to think about Mum.

"I miss my mum," said Grace.

"I think I want to go home."

Maya looked upset. "You can't go," she said.

"We haven't had the midnight feast!"

Then Grace saw Flop. She remembered that he was full of hugs from Mum. She hugged him tight and started to feel much better.

Maya's mum came in with some biscuits and a drink of milk. When they had finished, Grace felt sleepy. Before long, she was fast asleep with a smile on her face.

In the morning, Mum came to get Grace.

"It's time to go home," she called.

But Grace didn't come.

"I think they're upstairs hiding under

the bed," said Maya's mum.

"Why are you hiding?" asked Mum.

"I don't want to go home now," said Grace.

"We want to make a den," said Maya.

"Next time," laughed Maya's mum.

"What about another sleepover
at our house next week?" said Mum.

Grace and Maya smiled at each other.

"Yes please!" they said.

Story order

Look at these 5 pictures and captions.
Put the pictures in the right order
to retell the story.

1

Mum put Flop in Grace's bag.

2

Grace felt worried about the sleepover.

3

Grace packed her bag.

4

Grace didn't want to go home.

5

Grace and Maya had fun.

Independent Reading

This series is designed to provide an opportunity for your child to read on their own. These notes are written for you to help your child choose a book and to read it independently.

In school, your child's teacher will often be using reading books which have been banded to support the process of learning to read. Use the book band colour your child is reading in school to help you make a good choice. *The Sleepover* is a good choice for children reading at Gold Band in their classroom to read independently.

The aim of independent reading is to read this book with ease, so that your child enjoys the story and relates it to their own experiences.

About the book

Grace was very excited about having her first sleepover at her friend's house. But she starts to feel nervous before she goes. Mum reassures her that she is sure to have fun with Maya. And Grace has a great time until it is time to go to sleep. Luckily, her toy is on hand to help, and Grace soon wants to plan another sleepover.

Before reading

Help your child to learn how to make good choices by asking: "Why did you choose this book? Why do you think you will enjoy it?" Look at the cover together and ask: "What do you think the story will be about?" Ask your child to think of what they already know about sleepovers. Ask: "Do you think the girl is packing to go on a sleepover?" Remind your child that they can sound out the letters to make a word if they get stuck.

Decide together whether your child will read the story independently or read it aloud to you.

During reading

Remind your child of what they know and what they can do independently. If reading aloud, support your child if they hesitate or ask for help by telling the word. If reading to themselves, remind your child that they can come and ask for your help if stuck.

After reading

Support comprehension by asking your child to tell you about the story. Use the story order puzzle to encourage your child to retell the story in the right sequence, in their own words. The correct sequence can be found on the next page.

Help your child think about the messages in the book that go beyond the story and ask: "Why do you Grace feels worried? How does her mum help her to feel better?"

Give your child a chance to respond to the story: "What was it like when you went on a sleepover? (If your child has had a sleepover.) Or, do you think you would like to go on a sleepover? (If your child has not had a sleepover.)

Extending learning

Help your child reflect on the story and empathise with Grace, by asking: "What would you do if you and your friend wanted to play different things? How do you think that Grace and Maya feel when Grace gets worried before bedtime?"

In the classroom, your child's teacher may be teaching different kinds of sentences. There are many examples in this book that you could look at with your child, including statements, commands, exclamations and questions. Find these together and point out how the end punctuation can help us decide what kind of sentence it is.

Franklin Watts
First published in Great Britain in 2018
by The Watts Publishing Group

Series Editors: Jackie Hamley and Melanie Palmer
Series Advisors: Dr Sue Bodman and Glen Franklin
Series Designer: Peter Scoulding

A CIP catalogue record for this book is
available from the British Library.

ISBN 978 1 4451 6250 8 (hbk)
ISBN 978 1 4451 6252 2 (pbk)
ISBN 978 1 4451 6251 5 (library ebook)

Printed in China

Franklin Watts
An imprint of
Hachette Children's Group
Part of The Watts Publishing Group
Carmelite House
50 Victoria Embankment
London EC4Y 0DZ

An Hachette UK Company
www.hachette.co.uk

www.franklinwatts.co.uk

Answer to Story order: 3, 2, 1, 5, 4